5 Minute Bedtime Stories

5 Minute Bedtime Stories

LITTLE TIGER PRESS
London

Contents

Can't You Sleep, Dotty?

★ ★

Tim Warnes

Tick! Tick!

10

Dotty couldn't sleep.
It was her first night
in her new home.

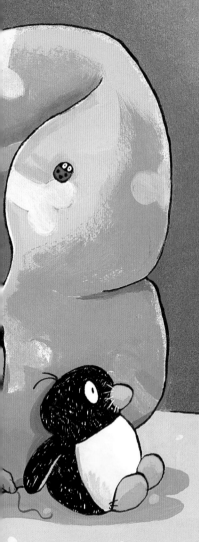

She tried sleeping
upside down.

She tried
snuggling up
to Penguin.

She even tried
lying on the floor.

AWOOOOOOOOOoooo

But still Dotty
couldn't sleep.

Dotty's howling woke up Pip the mouse.
"Can't you sleep, Dotty?" he asked.
"Perhaps you should try counting the stars
like I do."

But Dotty could
only count up to
one. *That* wasn't
enough to send
her to sleep.

What could she do next?

AWOOOOOOOOOO

Susie the bird was awake now. "Can't you sleep, Dotty?" she twittered. "I always have a little drink before I go to bed."

Chirp!
Chirp!

Dotty went to her bowl
and had a little drink.

Slurp!
Slurp!

But then she made
a little puddle.
Well *that*
didn't help!
What *could* Dotty
do to get to sleep?

AWOOOOOOOOoo..

Whiskers the rabbit had woken up, too. "Can't you sleep, Dotty?" he mumbled sleepily. "I hide away in my burrow at bedtime. That always works."

23

Dotty dived under her blanket so that only her bottom was showing. But it was all dark under there with no light at all.

Dotty was too scared to go to sleep.

Tommy the tortoise
poked his head from
out of his shell.

"Can't you sleep, Dotty?" he sighed.
"I like to sleep where it's bright and sunny."

Plod
Plod

Dotty liked that idea . . .

. . . and turned on her torch!

"Turn it off, Dotty!"
shouted all her friends.
"We can't get to sleep now!"

Poor Dotty was too
tired to try anything else.
Then Tommy had a great idea . . .

He helped Dotty into her bed.
What Dotty needed for the
first night in her new home was . . .

. . . to snuggle up among
all her new friends. Soon
they were all fast asleep.
Night night, Dotty.

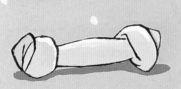

ZZZZZZZZZ

33

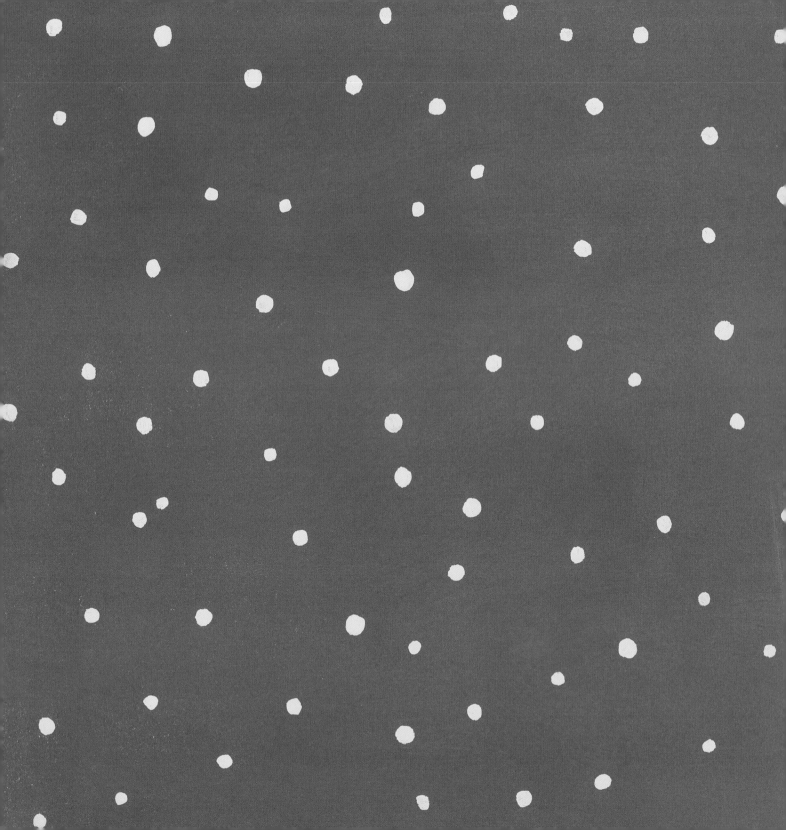

Night-Night, Newton

Rory Tyger

CREAK, CREAK, CRE-E-EAK!

Newton woke up suddenly. There was a funny noise somewhere in the room.

"Don't be frightened," he told Woffle. "There's always an explanation for everything."

He gave each of his toys a special cuddle so they wouldn't be scared.

CREAK, CREAK, CRE-E-EAK!

went the noise again.

Newton got out of bed and turned on the light.
He walked across the room . . .

"See, toys," he said. "There's nothing to be frightened of. It's only the wardrobe door!"

Newton went back to bed again.

FLAP! FLAP! FLAP!

What was that? Was it a ghost?

Once more Newton got out of bed. He wasn't really scared, but he took his bravest toy, Snappy, just in case. He tiptoed, very quietly, towards the noise.

FLAP! FLAP! FLAP!

"Of course!" said Newton . . .

"Just what I thought."
It was his bedroom curtains,
flapping in the breeze.
"I'll soon sort those out."

"You were very brave,
Snappy," he said, as
he closed the window.

SPLISH!

SPLASH!

SPLISH!

Another noise!

Newton looked outside. It wasn't raining.
Besides, the noise wasn't coming from outside.

Nor was it coming from his bedroom. What was it?

"Stay right there, you two," said Newton, "while I look around."

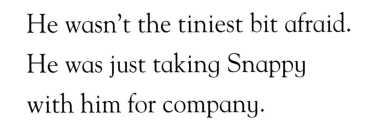

He wasn't the tiniest bit afraid. He was just taking Snappy with him for company.

Newton crept down the corridor. It was
very spooky, especially in the dark corners.

SPLISH! SPLASH! SPLISH!

went the noise.

Very, very quietly, Newton
opened the bathroom door . . .

"Of course, we knew it was the bathroom tap,
didn't we, Snappy," said Newton.

Newton turned off the tap, and
tiptoed back down the corridor.
"Shh," he said to Snappy, just
in case something in the dark
corners sprang out at them.

Before he got into bed,
Newton pulled back the
curtains – just to check. It
was very, very quiet outside.
  "No more funny noises,"
said Newton.

"You can go to sleep
  now," he told all his toys.

RUMBLE! RUMBLE! RUMBLE!

"Oh, no!" cried Newton. "What's that?"

Newton listened very hard. Not a sound.
He was just beginning to think he hadn't
heard anything at all when . . .

RUMBLE! RUMBLE! RUMBLE!

There it was again!

Newton peered under his bed.
Nothing there at all – except for an
old sweet he'd forgotten about.

"Don't worry," said Newton. "We'll
soon find out what it is."

RUMBLE!
Newton stood
very still.

RUMBLE!
Newton listened
very hard.

RUMBLE! went the noise.
And suddenly Newton knew
exactly what it was!

Newton padded downstairs, and into the kitchen.
He helped himself to a large glass of milk and two thick
slices of bread and honey. And now he could hear no

RUMBLE! RUMBLE! RUMBLE!

at all, because . . .

. . . the rumbling had been
his empty tummy!

Newton went upstairs again, and told his toys
about his rumbling tummy.

"There's always an explanation for everything,"
said Newton, as he climbed back into bed.
"Goodnight, everyone . . .

Sleep tight!"
SNORE, SNORE, SNORE!
went Newton.

What Are You Doing in My Bed?

David Bedford   Daniel Howarth

Kip the kitten had nowhere to sleep
on a dark and cold winter's night.
So he crept through a door . . .

. . . and curled up warm and
snug in somebody's bed.
Then out of the dark
Kip heard . . .

. . . whispers and hisses,
and soft feet padding
through the night.

Bright green eyes peered
in through the window,
and suddenly . . .

. . . one, two, three, four, five, six cats
came banging through the cat door!
They tumbled and skidded and rolled
across the floor, where they found . . .

. . . Kip!

"What are YOU doing in OUR bed?"
shouted the six angry cats.

"Your bed?" said Kip.
"But this bed's too small for
you. You'd never all fit!"
"Never fit?" said the cats.
"Just you watch . . ."

One, two, three cats curled up
neatly, head to tail . . .
then four, five, six cats
piled on top.

"See? There's no room
   for you," they said.
"You'd never fit."
      "Never fit?"
said Kip.
"Just you
   watch . . ."

Tottering and teetering,
  Kip carefully climbed on top.
"I'll sleep here," he said.
    "OK," the cats yawned.
"But don't fidget or snore."
  And they fell asleep in a heap.
    But suddenly, a big, deep,
growly voice said . . .

"WHAT ARE YOU
DOING IN MY BED?
SCRAM!"

The cats skitter-skattered round the room, but only found hard, cold places to sleep.

Harry the dog was comfy in his bed,
and he soon began to snore.
But then an icy wind whistled in
through the cat door, and Harry
awoke and shivered.

Kip whispered, "Follow me . . ."
and he quickly led six cold cats
across the floor . . .

. . . to the cosy bed.
"We'll keep you warm,"
said Kip.

"You'll never all fit," chattered Harry.

"Never fit?" said Kip. "Just you watch . . ."

Kip and Harry snored right through the night under their warm blanket of cats.

And they all fitted purr-fectly!

Bedtime, Little Ones!

Claire Freedman   Gail Yerrill

It's been such a happy day playing;
The setting sun glows golden red.
The little ones run home for supper,
For soon it will be time for bed.

Mummy Mouse smiles
at her children,
"Time for bed,
when you've
finished your teas!"
"We're not at all tired!"
the mice chorus,
But someone's asleep
in her cheese!

It's bathtime – five rabbits are splashing,
Having fun in their big bubbly tub!
"We love to splish-splosh!" they tell Mummy,
As she gives each small bunny a scrub.

Mummy Rabbit is
drying her bunnies,
And counting them,
"One, two, three, four . . ."

Then she giggles,
"Wait – somebody's missing!
There should be just
one bunny more!"

The little ones snuggle round Grandpa,
As he reads to them tales from his book.
"And another!" cries one little badger.
"There's a great story here,
Grandpa – look!"

Mummy Squirrel says,
"Bedtime, my babies,
Hear the sleepy-train
calling choo-choo!"
But one little squirrel's
not sleepy,
She still wants to
play peek-a-boo!

The little bears gaze at the night sky,
As silver bright stars start to peep.
"One, two, three, ZZZZ!" someone's snoring.
Star counting has sent him to sleep!

Little Rabbit is searching all over.
"Oh no!" he cries. "Where's Little Ted?
I must find my cuddly bear, Mummy,
I can't sleep without him in bed!"

All the animals have their own teddies,
To cuddle and snuggle up tight.
With each of their soft toys beside them,
They're sure to sleep soundly all night!

As Mummy Mouse
tucks up each baby,
She whispers, "Goodnight,
sleepy-head!"
Then Little Mouse
copies her Mummy,
And she tucks up her
own toy in bed.

The hedgehogs are drifting to sleep now,
As Daddy sings sweet lullabies,
But one little hedgehog is singing along,
"Tra-la-la! I love Daddy!" he cries.

Goodnight,
little badgers
and squirrels,
Sleep tight, little
bears and mice too,
Sweet dreams,
little hedgehogs
and rabbits,
And night-night
and sweet dreams
to YOU!

Bedtime
for Little Bears!

David Bedford   Caroline Pedler

Little Bear and his mother
had spent a long, sunny day
exploring in the snow.

"It's getting late," said Mother Bear. "It will soon be bedtime. Let's go home, Little Bear."

Little Bear flumped down in the snow and wiggled his tail. "I'm not sleepy," he said.

Mother Bear smiled. "Shall we have one last explore," she said, "and see who else is going to bed?"

Little Bear looked about. "Who else *is* going to bed?" he wondered.

Mother Bear stretched up tall to find out.

"Look there," she said.

"It's Little Owl!" said Little Bear.

"Little Owl likes to stretch her wings before bedtime, and feel the whisper of the soft night breeze in her feathers," said Mother Bear.

Little Bear scrambled onto his mother's shoulders.

"I like flying too!" he said.

As Mother Bear climbed to the top of a hill, Little Bear felt the wind whispering and tickling through his fur.

Then he saw someone else . . .

"Who's that?" said Little Bear, giggling. "And what's he doing?"

"Baby Hare is having a bath in the snow," said Mother Bear, "so that he's clean and drowsy, and ready for sleep."

"I like snow baths too," said
Little Bear. He dived into the
snow and plopped a big, soft
snowball on Mother
Bear's nose.

Little Bear and his mother
laughed as they flopped
down together in a heap.

"Are you sleepy now, Little
Bear?" his mother asked as
they lay together in the snow,
watching the first bright stars
twinkling in the sky.

Little Bear blinked his tired eyes as he tried not to yawn. "I want to see who else is going to bed," he said.

"We'll have to be quiet now," said Mother Bear. "Some little ones will already be asleep."

"Look over there," whispered Mother Bear.
"Little Fox likes being cuddled and snuggled
to sleep by his mother."

Little Bear pressed close against Mother Bear's
warm fur. "I like cuddles too," he said.

"We'll be home soon," said his mother softly.

But Little Bear had just seen somebody else . . .

"I can see whales!" he said, turning to look out
across the starlit sea.

"Little Whale likes his mother to sing him softly
to sleep," said Mother Bear.

Little Bear sat with his mother and watched the
whales swimming by until they were gone, leaving
only the soothing hum of their far-away song.

Then Little Bear climbed onto his mother's back, and as he was carried home he watched the colours that flickered and brushed across the sky, while his mother sang him a lullaby.

"I like songs too," he told his mother.

"And now," said Mother Bear very softly, "it's time for little bears to go to sleep."

Little Bear nestled into his mother's soft fur, and when she gave him a gentle kiss goodnight . . .

. . . Little Bear was
already fast asleep.

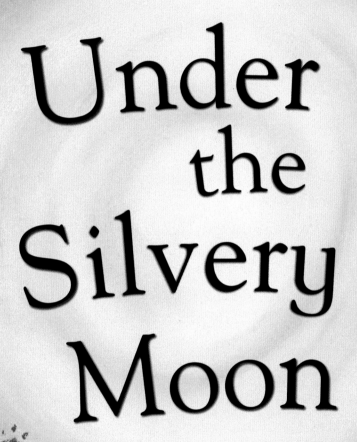

Under
the
Silvery
Moon

Colleen McKeown

The stars were shining brightly.
Little Kitten was in bed.
But up he sat, still wide awake,
"Sleep now," his mother said.

"But it's so noisy, I can't sleep!"
said Kitten, with a cry.
"It's just our friends," said Mother Cat.
"They're waking up nearby . . .

The tiny mice are playing;
    they explore the barn at night.
They skip and scamper here and there,
    beneath the warm lamplight.

Hush, Kitten, can you hear it,
that shuffling, snuffling sound?
The hedgehogs look for food to eat
along the moonlit ground.

152

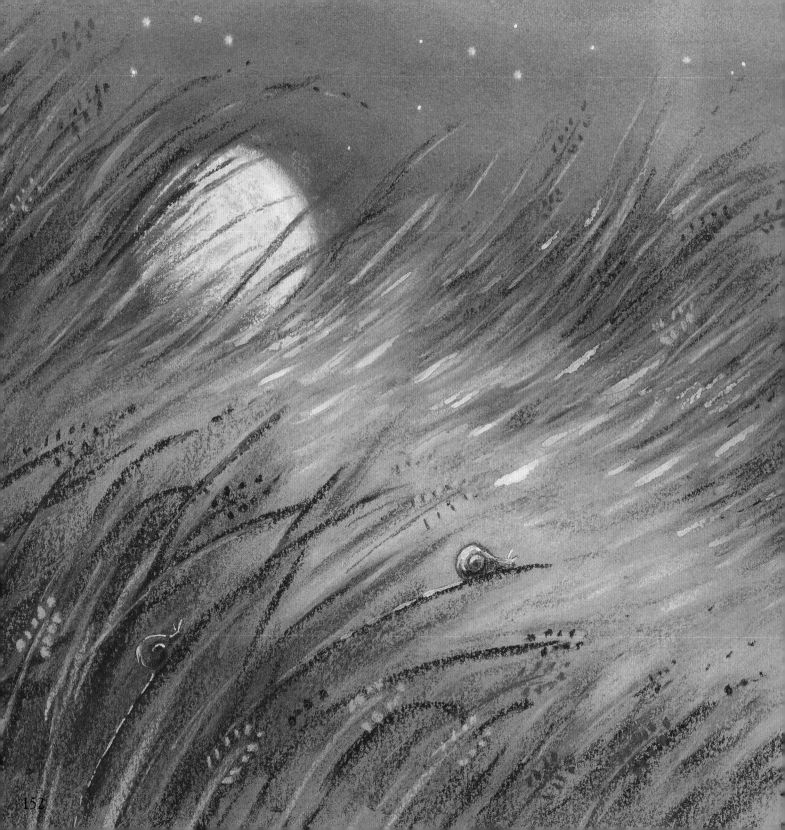

That cry you hear, so long and loud,
that distant, haunting tune,
Belongs to Fox who's up at night.
He's calling to the moon.

Around us swirls a summer song;
   it's whispered through the trees.
The evening wind is blowing
   through the softly rustling leaves.

Beyond the midnight meadow,
  where the air is soft and cool,
The frogs are gently croaking
  all around the moonlit pool.

Some creatures are not stirring;
they do not make a peep.
Like us, they've had a busy day,
and now they're fast asleep.

The badgers stretch their sturdy legs,
and blink into the dark.
'Good evening,' they are calling,
with a deep and playful bark.

The nimble hares are dancing;
their paws thump on the ground.
With joyful leaps they chase their tails
and spring and dart around.

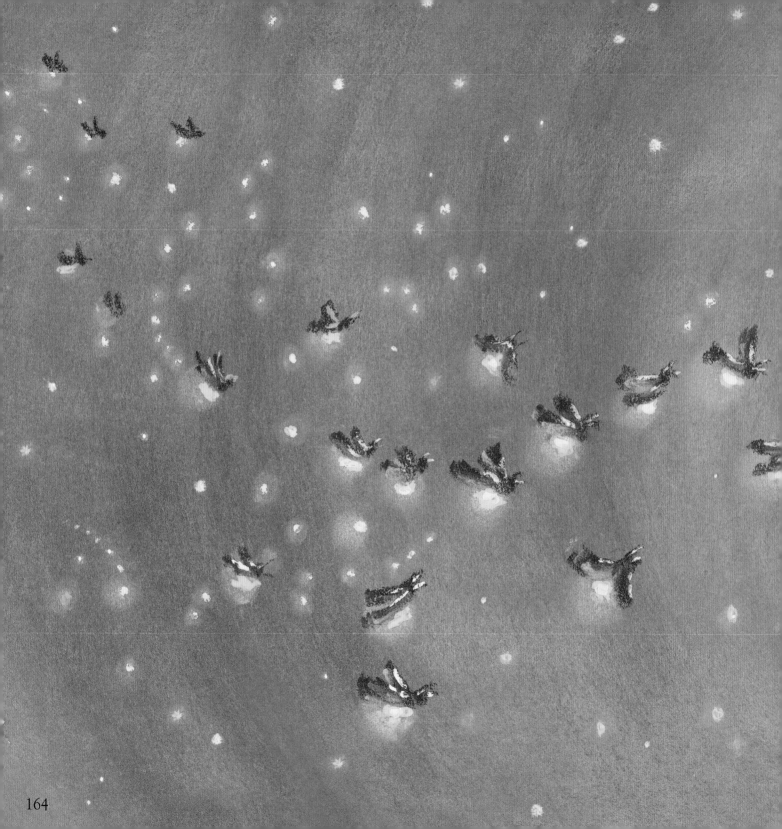

Something quiet and gentle
   lights up the dark, night skies.
Glowing warm and lovely
   are the dreamy fireflies.

Owl is hooting softly;
   across the stars she glides.
Soaring home towards the barn,
   upon the wind she rides.

And so you see, my little one,
  there's nothing you should fear.
Our friends' night-time adventures
  are all that you can hear."

Little Kitten closed his eyes
  and hugged his mother tight.
"It's time you went to sleep," she purred.
  "Sweet dreams, my love, goodnight."

169

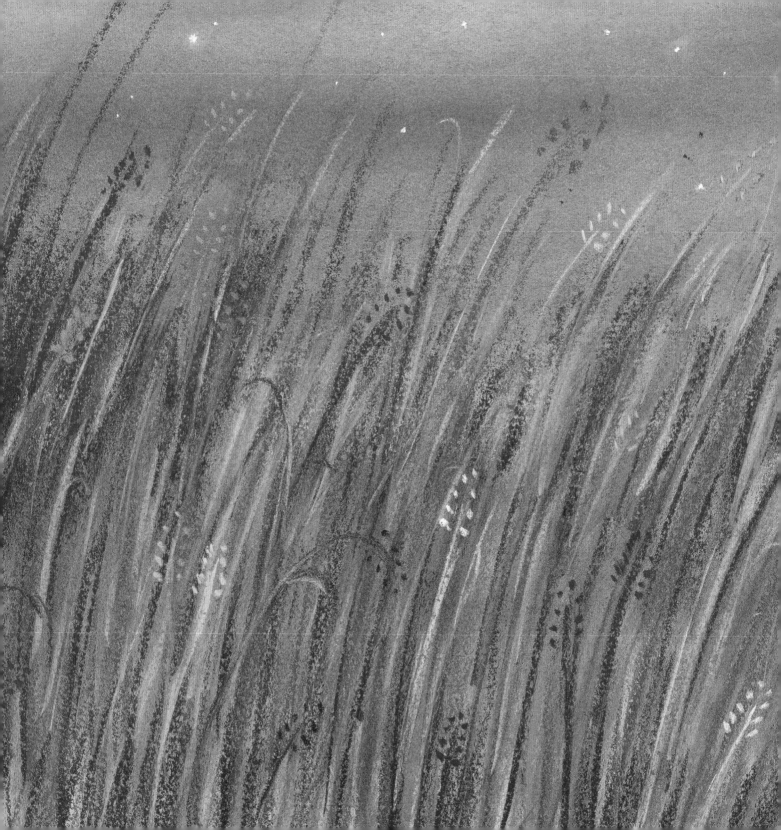

Time to Sleep, Alfie Bear!

Catherine Walters

"It's nearly bedtime, Alfie,"
called Mother Bear, gathering
up his baby brother and sister.
"Come along – time for your bath."

175

Alfie sat by the edge of the lake.
The fish leapt to catch the evening flies.
"Huh! The fish aren't going to bed,"
thought Alfie. "Why should I?"
It gave him an idea . . .

"Look! I'm a fish!" shouted Alfie. "I don't have to go to bed!"

He began to jump and dive and splash.

"Don't do that," sighed Mother Bear.

"The babies are getting too excited to sleep."

When they had all calmed down,
Mother Bear took them back home.
"Go and get some nice, cool grass
for bedding, Alfie," she said. "That
will help you sleep."

Alfie went outside and pulled up
a few pawfuls of grass.

Some owls were swooping through
the meadow.

"The owls aren't going to bed,"
thought Alfie. "Why should I?"

183

Alfie rushed back into the cave and began to flap his arms. "Look! I'm an owl!" he hooted. "I don't need to go to bed."

"Oh Alfie, stop that!" groaned Mother Bear. "Look, the babies are throwing all their lovely bedding around, too. None of you will have anywhere to sleep."

At last, Alfie and the babies were safely in bed.
"I think you need a nice, gentle song," said
Mother Bear. "Now, close your eyes."
Alfie wasn't listening. Outside, he could
hear wolves howling.
"The wolves aren't going to sleep,"
he thought. "Why should I?"

"Look, I'm a wolf! AAAAOOOW!" said Alfie.

"OW, OW, OW!" shrieked the babies.

"That's enough, Alfie," Mother Bear growled.

"I don't want any little wolves in the cave.

You can wait outside until the babies are asleep."

189

"Hooray!" cried Alfie, running outside.
He charged across the meadow howling,
"AAAAOOOW!"
Then, from somewhere close by,
someone answered him, "AAAAOOOW!"

Alfie jumped. There in front of him was
a wolf cub, with his family close by.

"Are you a wolf?" the cub asked. "You
sound like one, but you don't look like one."

"Are you sure you're a wolf?" called
a big, gruff voice . . .

". . . because you look like a little bear to me!"
"I'm a bear, I'm a bear!" shouted Alfie,
as Father Bear picked him up.
"Goodnight, little bear," called the
wolf cubs.

Father Bear snuggled Alfie into his fur.

"So you're a bear?" he said. "But are you a sleepy bear all ready for bed?"

"No," said Alfie. "I'm not . . ."

But before he could finish speaking, he had fallen fast asleep.

Hushabye Lily

Claire Freedman

John Bendall-Brunello

Night-time crept over the farmyard. But Lily pricked up her ears. "What's that quacking sound?" she asked.

"Hush now!" said Mother Rabbit. "It's only the ducks, resting in the tall reeds."

203

"Sorry, Lily!" Duck called out. "Are we keeping you awake? We were singing sleepy bedtime songs.

"Would you like me to sing you a song, too?"

"Yes, please!" Lily said.

So Duck puffed out his chest, shook out his feathers,
and sang the most beautiful duck lullaby he knew.
"That was lovely!" sighed Lily.
And without a sound, Duck waddled away,
back to the moonlit pond.

"Tu-whit, tu-whoo!"
hooted Owl.
　　"Hush!" whispered
Lily's mother.

TU-WHIT TU-WHOO

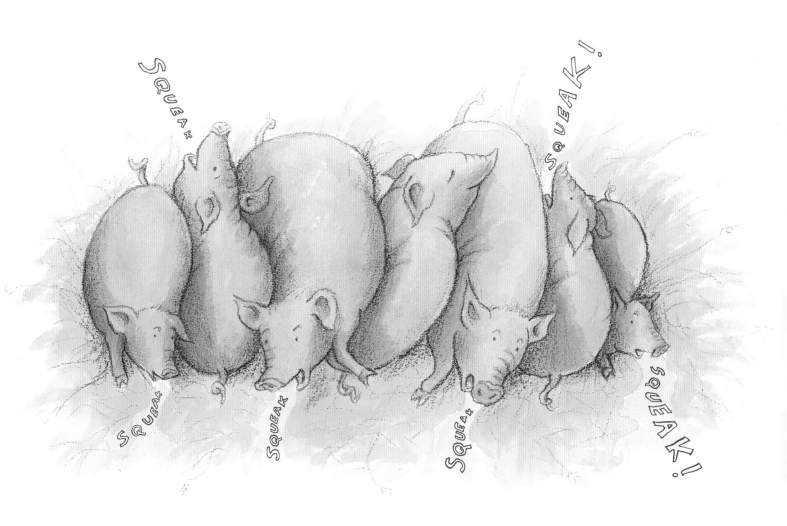

"Squeak, squeak," yawned the piglets.

"Shhh!" sighed Mother Rabbit. "Hush!"

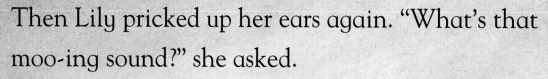

Then Lily pricked up her ears again. "What's that moo-ing sound?" she asked.

"Hush now!" said Mother Rabbit. "It's only the cows lowing in the cowshed."

"Sorry, Lily!" said Cow. "We were just telling each other bedtime stories. Would you like to hear a story, too?"

"Yes please!" said Lily.

So Cow told Lily her favourite sleepy bedtime tale.
"That was nice!" Lily yawned.
Cow lumbered back to the barn,
as quietly as she could.

"Miaow!" cried Cat,
  huddling her kittens together.

MIAOW

"Hee-haw!" brayed Donkey,
turning in his sleep.
"Shhh!" sighed Lily's mother.
"Hush now!"

215

Then Lily pricked up her ears once more.

"What's that clucking sound?" she asked.

"It's only the hens hiding in the haystacks," said Mother Rabbit.

"Sorry, Lily!" called out Hen. "We were collecting straw for our beds. Would you like some too?"

"Oooh yes!" said Lily.

So Hen brought back a beakful of
straw and tucked it under Lily's head.
"That's cosy," said Lily, sleepily.
Then Hen crept off softly to the
hen coop, on tiptoes.

"Shhh!" hushed the ducks
to the rippling reeds.

"Shhh!" hushed the cows
to the leaves on the trees.

221

"Shhh!" hushed the hens
to the whispering wind.

Ssshhhh

"Hush now, Lily!" whispered Mother Rabbit,
and she snuggled up against her little one.
The moon hid behind the clouds.
All was quiet and still, until . . .

. . . down in the stable,

Little Foal pricked up his ears.

"What's that whistling sound?" he asked.

"Shhh, go back to sleep!" his mother whispered.

"It's only little Lily snoring!"

Goodnight, Little Hare

Sheridan Cain

Sally Percy

Under the silvery moon, Little Hare
lay with eyes tightly shut. For his
blanket he had the sky, and the soft
hay formed his bed.

"Goodnight, Little Hare," Mother Hare
whispered.

Just then, Mole happened by. "You cannot leave your baby there," he said. "The farmer cuts the hay at dawn."

"But what can I do?" asked Mother Hare. "Where can Little Hare sleep?"

"You should dig a hole!" said Mole.

So Mother Hare began to dig.

She scraped and scraped
at the soft, brown earth, until
the hole was big and deep. Then
she carried Little Hare to his new bed.

But Little Hare did not
like it. "Mama," he cried.
"It's so dark and I
cannot sleep."

235

"Mother Hare," said Badger, who was bumbling along, "you cannot leave your baby in the dark."

"But where can Little Hare sleep?"
asked Mother Hare.
"You should cover him in a
bed of leaves," said Badger.

So Mother Hare hurried
and she scurried.

She made a soft, round pile with
the leaves. Then she carried Little
Hare to his new bed.

But Little Hare did not like it.

"Mama," he cried. "I don't like the crinkly-crackly noise my new bed makes."

Blackbird heard Little Hare's cry from his tree.

"Mother Hare," he said, "you cannot leave your baby there."

"But where can Little Hare sleep?" asked Mother Hare.

"What you need is a nest up high," said Blackbird.

So Mother Hare placed
Little Hare in an empty
bird's nest.

But Little Hare did not like it.
"Mama," he cried, looking down,
"it's high up here and I might
fall out."

So Mother Hare carried Little Hare down again. She did not know what to do. "Oh dear," she sighed. "How can I find the right bed for Little Hare?"

Owl was watching
from his perch.

"Don't you remember how your mother kept you safe when *you* were young?" he said.

Mother Hare remembered how the
sky had been her blanket and the soft,
golden hay had been her bed.

She remembered how, from dusk to dawn,
her mother had watched over her.

The sun was just rising. Mother Hare's eyes became bright. The farmer had come early, and the hay was cut.

It was quite safe there now.

251

Mother Hare carried Little Hare back to his old bed and laid him gently down.

"Mama," said Little Hare.
"This is my own bed, and I
like it."

Then everyone whispered,
"Goodnight, Little Hare!"

Goodnight, Sleep Tight!

Claire Freedman
Rory Tyger

One night, Grandma
was looking after Archie.

"Aren't you sleepy yet?"
she asked.

"No!" replied Archie.
"I don't feel sleepy at all!"

"Have you got all your
favourite friends to cuddle?
They might help you feel
sleepy," Grandma said.

"I've got Tiger and Rabbit,
but where's Elephant?"
said Archie.

"Here he is," said
Grandma, tucking him
in nice and snug.

But Archie still wasn't
sleepy.

"How about some nice
warm milk?" said
Grandma.

Archie drank his milk, but he still didn't feel sleepy.

"Please can we watch the fireflies, Grandma?" he said. "That'll make me sleepy."

Grandma wrapped Archie in his cosy blanket and together they watched the dancing fireflies. Archie tried to count them but it didn't make him feel sleepy.

"I'm still wide awake, Grandma!" he said. "Can you sing me a lullaby, please?"

Grandma sang some
of Archie's favourite
songs. Archie closed his eyes
and listened.

"I'm still wide awake,
Grandma," he whispered.

"Let me rock you in my arms,"
Grandma said.

So Grandma rocked Archie
gently in her arms, all the way
down to the apple garden.
Archie felt safe and warm,
but he didn't feel sleepy.

"Grandma, I'm *still* wide awake!"
he said. "Will you tell me a story,
please? Listening to stories
makes me feel sleepy."

Grandma sat down comfortably,
and Archie snuggled up close
to her.

She told him stories
about all the naughty
things his mummy
had done when
she was little
– just like him.

"Your mummy
never felt sleepy
at bedtime either,"
Grandma said.

Grandma carried Archie back inside.
She smiled a secret smile as she
remembered putting Archie's
mummy to bed when she
was little.

Grandma tucked
Archie up in bed.
"I used to tuck your mummy
up in bed, with the blankets pulled
right up to her nose – like this!"
said Grandma.

"Then I'd stroke
the top of
Mummy's
forehead
– like this,"
Grandma said.

Very gently she stroked the top of Archie's forehead.

"And I'd give her a very special
goodnight kiss," said Grandma.
Grandma gave Archie
a special goodnight kiss.

278

"That's right, Grandma," said Archie
with a big yawn. "And then she says,
'Goodnight, sleep tight!'"

"That's right, Archie," said Grandma . . .

And before Grandma could
even say "Goodnight, sleep tight",
Archie was fast asleep!

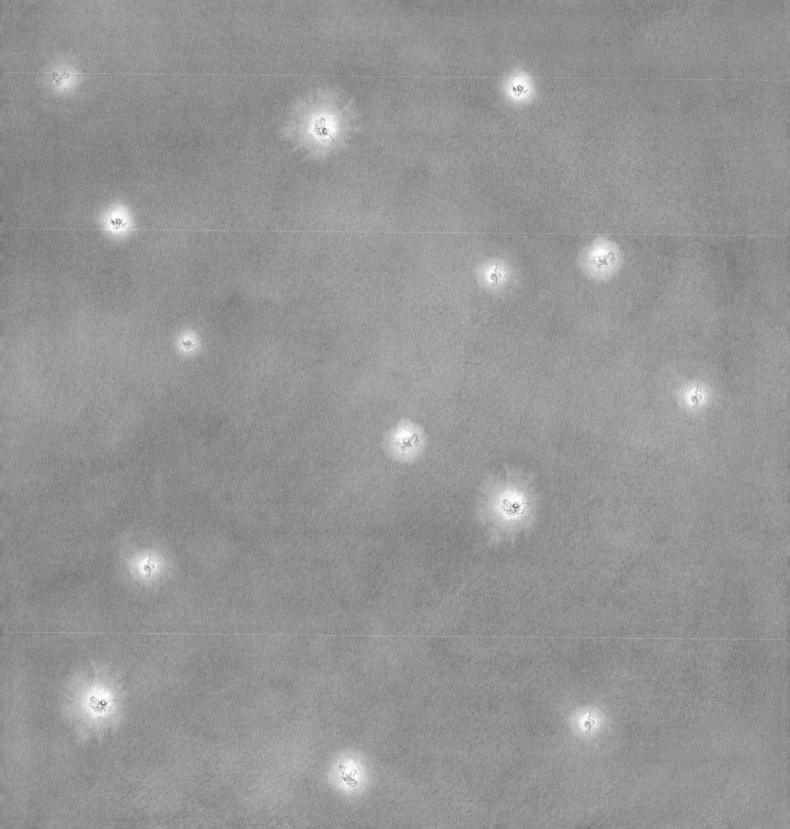

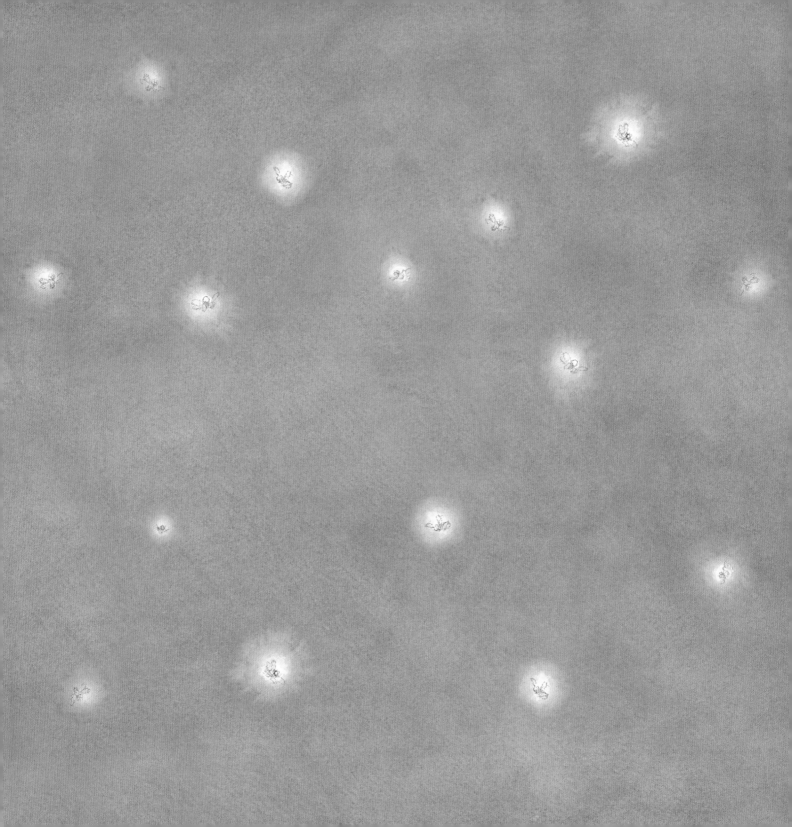

5 MINUTE BEDTIME STORIES

LITTLE TIGER PRESS
1 The Coda Centre,
189 Munster Road,
London SW6 6AW
www.littletiger.co.uk

First published in Great Britain 2012

Printed in China

LTP/1800/0870/0114

ISBN 978-1-84895-551-6

2 4 6 8 10 9 7 5 3

GOODNIGHT, LITTLE HARE

Sheridan Cain
Illustrated by Sally Percy

First published in Great Britain 1999
by Little Tiger Press

Text copyright © Sheridan Cain 1999
Illustrations copyright © Sally Percy 1999

GOODNIGHT, SLEEP TIGHT!

Claire Freedman
Illustrated by Rory Tyger

First published in Great Britain 2003
by Little Tiger Press

Text copyright © Claire Freedman 2003
Illustrations copyright © Rory Tyger 2003